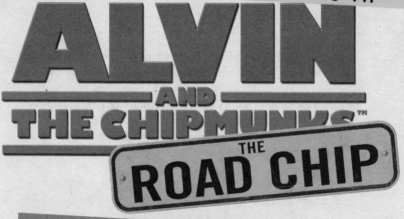

JUNIOR NOVELIZATION

Adapted by Kate Howard
from the screenplay by Randi Mayem Singer
and Adam Sztykiel

Based upon the characters Alvin and
the Chipmunks
created by Ross Bagdasarian
and the Chipettes
created by Janice Karman

SCHOLASTIC INC.

Published by Scholastic Inc., *Publishers since 1920.* SCHOLASTIC and
associated logos are trademarks and/or registered trademarks of
Scholastic Inc.

ISBN 978-0-545-93433-6

10 9 8 7 6 5 4 3 2 1   16 17 18 19 20

Printed in the U.S.A   40
First printing December 2015
Book design by Rick DeMonico

Dave's birthday message, take one!" Alvin squeezed in next to his brothers, Simon and Theodore, and held up his cell phone. He hit the RECORD button.

All three chipmunks smiled at the camera. "Happy birthday, Dave!"

"Dave," began Alvin, hamming it up for the camera. Alvin—one of the famous singing

Chipmunks—had had more time on-screen than most chipmunks. More screen time than most *people*, too. "Dave, we know how hard you've been working on Ashley's album, so we thought it would be fun to surprise you with a little party."

Brittany, one of the three Chipettes, popped up behind the Chipmunks. "Hey!" she said. "I thought you said this was a going-away party for us."

Alvin yelled, *"Cut!"* and then grinned at Brittany. "Take two," he said, hitting the RECORD button again. "Dave, to celebrate your birthday *and* the Chipettes leaving town to guest-judge on *American Idol*, we thought we'd throw a small party—" Alvin paused the video. There was a call coming in. He glanced at the caller ID. "Hold on, that's the DJ."

"DJ?" Simon gasped. He shook his head as a sound crew carried equipment into Dave's house.

Alvin ignored him and pressed RECORD again. "Happy birthday, Dave! We thought it would be fun to surprise you with a *medium-sized party . . .*"

Simon glanced out the window and then cut off his brother again. "Alvin, did you hire someone to build a half-pipe in the backyard?!"

"Of course not." Alvin grinned mischievously. "The party planner did."

"You hired a party planner?!" Simon shrieked. They had discussed a small party for Dave's birthday. This was turning into something else altogether. Sometimes Alvin got a little carried away.

"No, he did not hire a *party planner*," said a voice in the doorway. It was a woman Simon had never seen before.

"Oh, thank goodness," said Simon.

"Anyone can plan a *party*," the woman went on. "I'm an *event* planner. A party planner gets a cake. An *event planner* gets a fireworks show that will put the Fourth of July to shame!"

Alvin rubbed his paws together. "Fireworks?!"

"No!" yelled Simon. "No fireworks."

"No fireworks," agreed the event planner. Under her breath, she added, "For now. I'm still working on the permit."

Alvin grinned. Dave's birthday party was going to be epic!

A few hours later, the party was in full swing. There was just one thing left to do: The Chipmunks had to finish recording their video message. "Happy birthday, Dave!" Theodore said, starting another take. He turned so the phone was facing away from the party.

"Dave, it's all good," Alvin promised. "As you can see, it's just us. Nothing too crazy—" He broke off. Theodore had accidentally hit the FLIP button. The Chipmunks disappeared, and the whole party popped into view. "Okay, fine, we're throwing you a pretty *big* party," Alvin admitted.

Simon popped up behind Alvin. "Dave, it's huge, and I'm sorry. Alvin said 'a few close friends,' but . . ." Clearly, there were more than a few friends in Dave's backyard—there were friends, celebrities, and even random strangers. The whole place was a madhouse, and Simon knew Dave was going to kill them. "Uh, Dave?" he said. "There's no way to sugarcoat it—the cops are here."

Alvin beamed at the camera. "Yeah, and they're having a blast!" He turned the phone around again—just in time to catch the cops playing limbo with the Chipettes.

Two police officers waved madly at the camera. "Happy birthday, Dave!"

"Bottom line," Alvin said, smiling earnestly into the phone, "you deserve a big party."

Simon shrugged. "Dave, as much as I hate to admit it, Alvin's right. You bought a new house, you gave up songwriting to start producing, and we know you did all that for us. So, thanks."

"We love you, Dave!" cheered Theodore. "Happy birthday!"

A few minutes later, the Chipmunks' birthday message was in the can. Everyone was having fun at Dave's birthday party. In fact, they had a line of guests waiting to get in. "No more," Simon announced. "Sorry! We're already a hundred people over the fire code."

He stepped aside to let a flock of pizza delivery guys—carrying thirty cheese pizzas—into the backyard. Behind them, the band began to rock out. Nearby, the Chipettes and Simon watched as skateboarders launched themselves off the skate ramp and into the pool.

"Is that safe?" Jeanette asked Simon.

Simon sighed. Simon didn't really *do* danger. "No, it is not." Simon scrambled up the half-pipe and grabbed a girl's board out of her hand. "Sorry, but the launch ramp is closed. This is a lawsuit waiting to happen."

A few people spotted Simon standing at the top of the ramp. They began to chant, "Si-mon! Si-mon! Si-mon!"

Simon held up his paw and chuckled. "No, no, I'm not going. I was just explaining to this young lady that it's dangerous, and . . ." The crowd continued to chant louder and louder. Finally, Simon nodded. "Okay, I'll do just one." He gritted his teeth and went for it. Screaming, he dropped onto the ramp, rode it all the way down, and plunged into the pool.

It was totally awesome! Simon pumped his fist. "I'm going again!"

The crowd cheered. Alvin cranked the music up, leading everyone in a crazy dance.

In all the commotion, no one noticed that Dave—the guest of honor—had returned home. And he did *not* look happy about his surprise party.

"Let me hear you out there!" Alvin yelled out to the crowd. "I say *party*, you say *ALVIN!* Party!"

"ALVIN!" the whole party screamed.

At the same time, Dave yelled, *"Al-vin!"*

"Party!" Alvin chanted again.

"ALVIN!" the guests and Dave yelled together.

"Party!" shouted Alvin one more time.

Frustrated, Dave pulled the plug on the music. The crowd went quiet, except for Dave and one other guy who was really into the chant. He and Dave both shouted, "Alllllllll-*viiiiiin!*"

"Dave!" Alvin said, shocked. From up onstage, he grinned sheepishly. "Uh . . . surprise?"

CHAPTER 2

D ave's house was an absolute disaster. "Party's over," Dave said grumpily, ushering people out the front door. "Thanks for coming."

Once the last guests were gone, Alvin asked, "Were you surprised?"

"No!" Dave growled. "And do you know

why I wasn't surprised? Because hashtag 'Dave's Party' was trending on Twitter!"

"Nice!" Alvin said happily. He cringed when he saw Dave's angry expression. "I mean . . . sorry?"

"I know my work schedule is tough," Dave said, slumping down into a chair. "But I was hoping you guys were old enough to take care of yourselves. I guess you're not mature enough for that."

Alvin shook his head somberly. "Dave, we are very mature."

"Look," Dave said, sighing heavily. "I don't expect you to fully understand, but I'm trying to start a new chapter in my life. A more stable chapter, where you guys aren't performing in a different city every night. The new house and the new job are a part of that."

"But we love to perform!" Simon protested.

"And you can," Dave said. "Join the debate team. Sign up for the school play."

"You didn't let him finish," Alvin cut in. "The rest of Simon's sentence was '. . . to packed clubs and arenas.' "

"You guys can go back to that," said Dave. "Just not now. I want you to have a few years as normal kids."

"But we're not 'normal kids,' Dave," said Theodore.

"Yeah," Alvin said. "We're multiplatinum singing chipmunks."

"Right now, you're acting like a bunch of animals who threw a giant house party without my permission," grumbled Dave.

"We're sorry, Dave," said Simon. "We shouldn't have surprised you like this."

"Does this mean no miniature golf tomorrow?" Theodore asked.

"You mean the low-key thing that I planned for my birthday?" Dave said. "It should. And normally it would."

"But you're going to give us one last chance?" Alvin asked hopefully. He grinned. "I mean, our one-hundred-fifty-eighth chance?"

Dave shook his head. "Selfishly, I want to spend some time with you guys before Ashley's album release party in Miami."

"We're going to Miami?!" Alvin asked, jumping up and down. "Theodore, get our Speedos!"

"Guys, guys, guys," Dave said, holding up a hand. "Put your Speedos away. It's just me. I only get a 'plus one,' and it wouldn't be fair to pick favorites."

Alvin hopped up on Dave's shoulder and whispered, "Your secret is safe with me, Dave. We both know I'm your favorite."

Dave glared at him.

"Okay, *tied* for favorite? You don't even have to say with who," Alvin added. "Blink once for Theodore, twice for Simon."

Dave glared even harder.

Alvin hopped down. "Got it. No favorites."

The next morning, Dave and the Chipmunks celebrated Dave's birthday *Dave's* way—with a nice, quiet round of minigolf.

"This is what it's all about," Alvin said, lining up his shot. "Just four dudes, playing some golf."

"That reminds me," Dave said. "I hope it's okay, but I invited a friend to join us."

"Ooh," Simon cooed. "Is this the famous Samantha we've been hearing so much about?"

Dave blushed. "It is. And it's starting to feel kinda serious, so I thought it was time for an introduction."

"You must really like this girl, Dave," said Alvin.

"I do." Dave nodded and looked across the minigolf course. "That's her now. How do I look?"

Alvin looked Dave up and down and shrugged. "Eh."

Simon groaned. "Alvin, this is no time for honesty."

Theodore gave Dave a thumbs-up. "You look great, Dave! That sweater makes you look like a cozy grandpa."

Dave patted his sweater and took a deep breath. "Guys, this is going down as one of the worst pep talks ever." He walked over to greet Samantha, then turned to call over his shoulder, "Alvin . . . just please behave."

While they waited, the guys practiced their shots. Simon, especially, took minigolf seriously. "Simon gets set," he said, lining up his putt. "The pressure is mounting, as if he knows he's a hole in one away from becoming the first chip-munk to win the Masters." He swung back, and then knocked his ball straight toward the hole. Pumping his fist, Simon cheered, "It's in the ho—"

Just then, a ratty shoe stepped in front of the hole, blocking the ball from going in. "Hey!"

"That's my brother's ball!" Theodore squeaked.

"This ball?" asked the shoe's owner. It was a smirking teenage boy holding a skateboard. He was clearly getting a kick out of ruining the Chipmunks' game. "No, this is my ball."

"I just hit it!" Simon argued.

"Tell you what," said the kid. "Let's compro-mise and call it *no one's* ball." He picked up the ball and threw it.

"I'm warning you," Alvin hissed at him. "You mess with one of us, you mess with all of us!"

"Ooh," the boy teased. He grabbed Theodore and attached him to a little windmill

15

that was part of the course. Then he grinned. "I'm terrified. What are you gonna do to me?"

Theodore flapped his arms. "We will continue this conversation when I'm back!" The windmill spun Theodore up and away.

"Whatever," Simon said. "Let him keep the ball."

"Si's right," agreed Alvin. "You're not worth it." He turned away from the boy, seething.

Dave and Samantha strolled up then. "Guys," Dave said. "I'd like you to meet Samantha. Sam, these are my boys."

"We've heard a lot about you," said Alvin. "*Enchanté.*"

Samantha smiled at him. "I can tell you're trouble."

Alvin grinned back at her. "If by *trouble*, you mean 'irresistible,' then guilty as charged."

"And this is Simon," Dave said. "In fact, you two are the smartest people I know."

"So you're a doctor?" Simon asked.

"I am," said Samantha. "Did Dave mention that?"

Simon shook his head. "No, you're wearing a stethoscope."

"And last," said Dave, grabbing Theodore off the still-spinning windmill. "But definitely not least. He might be the smallest, but he's got the biggest heart in the world. This is Theodore."

"It's so nice to finally meet you guys," Samantha said. "And it's great you've already met my son, Miles."

The guys followed her finger. She was pointing to the kid. The kid with the shoe. The horrible, awful teenager.

"Son?" squeaked Alvin.

"We thought this was the perfect place for you guys to get to know one another a little bit," Samantha added.

For the rest of the afternoon, the Chipmunks

were forced to play with Miles while Dave and Samantha made goo-goo eyes at each other. Every time Dave or Samantha was watching, Miles pretended to be nice. But when they weren't? Miles did everything he could to torture the Chipmunks. He even tried to sell Theodore!

"Twenty bucks seems like a lot of money for a chipmunk," a little kid told Miles.

"He's a talking chipmunk," Miles pointed out. "Go on, plump and juicy, say something."

"I also sing," Theodore said.

The little kid handed over a twenty and snatched Theodore out of Miles's hands.

"Hey," Alvin protested. "Give us back our brother!"

The little kid shook his head. "I just paid twenty bucks for him."

"He wasn't for sale!" yelled Simon.

Miles shrugged. "Well, no one told me that."

"I hope you're happy, Theodore," Alvin said as he handed the little kid some of his cash. "That was all of our allowance."

"Hey, fellas!" Dave called to them. "Great news. You get to hang with Miles all day. Samantha just got paged by the hospital, so I'm gonna take the four of you to the studio with me."

"Are you sure it isn't any trouble?" Samantha asked.

"Of course not," Dave said. "It'll be fun to have a little guys' time."

The Chipmunks glared at Miles.

Miles glared back.

Half an hour later, it was clear their afternoon at the studio was going to be anything but fun. "I didn't realize how boring it is to be on this side of the glass," Alvin said, resting his cheek on his fist. The guys had been watching

Ashley Grey, one of the world's biggest pop stars, sing the same song over and over and over again.

"Why aren't you guys in there?" Miles asked with a sneer. "I thought you were, like, super-famous or something."

"One day we're throwing back pink lemonades on Diddy's yacht in Saint-Tropez, and the next we're eating stale chips you find in the couch," Simon said wistfully.

Theodore pulled a stale chip out of the couch. "I miss it," he said sadly. He went to pop the chip in his mouth.

But Dave's sound engineer, Barry, stopped him. "Sorry, Theodore. Couch chips are for talent only."

"Really, Barry?" whined Theodore.

Barry blinked. "All right, you can keep the chip. Just don't tell anyone, okay?"

Theodore munched on the stale chip, thinking about how much better life had been when he was one of the singing sensations who got to eat the good chips. Those were the days . . . If only there were some way to get a little of that excitement back.

CHAPTER 3

Later that night, Dave and Samantha enjoyed a quiet dinner together—just the two of them.

"Well, we did it," said Samantha. "We successfully introduced our kids to one another."

"And then you performed open heart surgery," Dave added. "I don't know how you do it."

"After being a single mom and a med student,

I could do this in my sleep," Samantha said. "But my life is a little more hectic than I'd like to admit."

"I get it," Dave said. "When stuff is going well at work, I'm missing out as a parent. But when I'm being a great dad, I'm dropping the ball at work."

Samantha nodded. "So, I have to ask . . . are the boys, like, your adopted kids, or how does that work, exactly?"

"I don't know," Dave said. "I've never really thought about it. It's nothing official, they're just . . . my boys."

"They're lucky to have you."

Dave smiled at her. He really liked this girl! "Crazy idea . . . what are you doing this weekend, and have you ever been to Miami?"

When he got home that night, Dave found the Chipmunks watching the Chipettes on TV. "Sorry

I'm late, fellas," he said. "I had to pick something up on the way home." He dropped a blue bag on the counter and disappeared inside his room.

"Ooh!" Theodore said, hopping up onto the counter. "Leftovers!" He dug through the bag and pulled out a small box. He sniffed it, but there was no sign of food. He popped it open, and his eyes went wide. "Hey guys, look what I found."

Alvin and Simon scampered over. It was a ring box. And inside the box, there was a huge ring.

"Whoa," said Alvin. "That is a serious rock. Wait, this is an engagement ring. Dave is going to ask Samantha to marry him!"

"We don't know that," Simon said. "They've only been together a few months. You're probably overreacting."

"Here comes Dave!" Theodore whispered.

"Act casual," warned Alvin. He quickly stuffed the ring box back into the bag.

Dave came back into the room and narrowed his eyes. The Chipmunks looked *very* guilty. "What are you guys doing?"

"Uh, yoga?" Alvin said, stretching. "Downward 'munk."

Dave shook his head. "Well, I hope you guys liked Samantha, because I think she's going to become a pretty big part of my life." Alvin nudged Simon, who flinched. Dave didn't notice. "Oh! And good news, my plus-one isn't going to waste. Samantha is coming with me to Miami." He grabbed the blue bag off the counter, then headed back into his room.

"I've always wanted a mom," Theodore said quietly.

"It would be nice to have a female presence in our lives," agreed Simon.

But Alvin groaned. "Guys, if Samantha is our mom, that makes Miles . . ."

"Our brother!" Simon gasped.

Theodore grabbed a paper bag and started breathing into it—in, out, in, out. Through the bag he asked, "What are we gonna do?"

"I'll tell you what we're gonna do," said Alvin. "We're gonna get that ring. No ring, no proposal. No proposal, no marriage. No marriage, no Miles. I don't know about you guys, but I like this family the way it is."

"Me too," Theodore moaned.

Many hours later, when Dave was fast asleep, the Chipmunks snuck into Dave's room. They were on a mission. A mission to steal the ring!

"Theodore, you keep an eye on Dave," said Alvin. "Si and I will get the ring."

While Theodore kept watch, Simon and Alvin searched for the blue bag. But just as Simon grabbed the bag with the ring, Dave woke up. Theodore, who had been sitting on Dave's chest, jumped up and yelled, "Morning, Dave!"

"Yeah," Simon chimed in, tossing the bag to Alvin. "Morning, Dave!"

Dave stretched and yawned. "What are you guys doing in here?"

Alvin tossed the ring bag under Dave's bed for safekeeping, and then smiled sweetly. "We just want to spend as much time as possible with you before you leave for Miami."

"Great," Dave said, climbing out of bed. "I'll make breakfast."

After breakfast, Dave got his things together for his trip. "Ms. Price from next door is going to peek in on you guys, just to make sure you're okay," he told the boys.

"We'll be fine," Alvin promised. "We don't need anyone checking in on us."

"Sorry, guys," Dave said. "But after the party, I don't feel real comfortable leaving you totally unsupervised." The doorbell rang. "That must be Samantha and Miles."

"Miles?" Alvin said.

"Yeah," Dave told him. "He's going to stay with you guys while we're gone."

"So you don't feel comfortable leaving us alone," said Simon, "but you're okay leaving us with that psychopath?"

Dave chuckled. "He's a good kid. And I think spending a few days with him will be a great bonding experience for you guys."

"Uh, I'm pretty sure Miles would interpret 'bonding experience' as supergluing us together," whispered Simon.

Dave flung open the door. "Welcome, Miles! Make yourself at home. *Mi casa, su casa.*"

Speaking perfect Spanish, Miles said, "Thank you, Dave. That's very generous of you to open your home."

"Wow!" Dave said. "That's impressive. I actually don't speak Spanish."

Simon leaned toward Miles and said in

Spanish, "I also speak Spanish. And you're not fooling anyone with your good-boy routine."

Miles smiled at him as he replied in Spanish, "I'm fooling everyone. They have no idea I'm gonna make you my personal servant while they're gone."

Dave watched Miles and Simon chatting and he beamed. "Look at those two Don Juans, chit-chattin' *en español*. I love it!" He picked up his bags and added, "You guys have a great weekend! I'll FaceTime you every night at eight, so make sure you have your phones on you." As he and Samantha walked out the door, Dave turned back and smiled. "I can feel the bonding happening!"

Miles smiled at him sweetly. "Oh, we're gonna do tons of bonding."

As the door closed, he turned to the Chipmunks. "Where's the superglue?"

iles!" Alvin called, pounding on a window. "If we're gonna make this work, we need to talk."

Miles closed his eyes. "I feel like it's working great."

Theodore pounded on the window, too. Miles had locked them out—of their own house!—hours ago. "You can't shut us out forever."

"He means emotionally," Simon explained. "But I want to focus on how you *actually* shut us out of our own home. I have to use the bathroom."

Miles looked out the window and rolled his eyes. "Trust me, guys. Dave and my mom are temporary."

"If by *temporary* you mean 'till death do they part,' then yeah, totally temporary," Simon said.

Miles looked up. "What are you talking about?"

"He's talking about marriage, Miles," said Alvin. "Wedding bells. Let us in and we'll show you."

Reluctantly, Miles opened the window. Alvin slid the blue bag out from under Dave's bed. Miles pulled a handful of tissue paper out of the bag. "A bag of tissue. Wow. Scandalous."

"It's gone," Simon said, pawing through the

pile of loose tissue paper. "He must have packed the ring before bed last night. He's gonna propose to Samantha in Miami!"

"So?" Miles spat. "You think we're gonna become, like, this big happy family? Here's the good news: If my mom and Dave do get married, they'll want to start their own family. And you're not even Dave's real sons. You're just three chipmunks he calls his kids, so you'll be the first to go."

"We're Dave's family," Alvin told him.

Miles smirked. "And I'm sure Dave has convinced himself it will all work out. Stepkids and stepmunks and new kids . . . a big, crazy, mixed family. But he'll change his tune. Before you know it, you'll be back in the forest."

"Dave wouldn't do that to us!" Theodore said, tears in his eyes.

"*Dave wouldn't do that to us,*" Miles said, mocking Theodore. "Open your eyes; he already has. Why is my mom in Miami and you guys aren't?"

Alvin pulled his brothers aside. "I don't want Miles to be right any more than you guys do, but it all lines up: new job, new house, new girlfriend . . . new family."

Alvin crossed his arms and faced Miles. "Here's the deal, Miles. You don't like us and we don't like you. We are enemies with a common goal. I say we all go to Miami, stop this proposal, and then we never have to see each other again."

Miles nodded. "I can't get you Chipmunks out of my life fast enough."

Alvin nodded back. "That's the smartest thing you've said since we met you."

Later that afternoon, Miles and the Chipmunks left Dave's house with a plan (sort of) and a common goal: to stop Dave from proposing.

"I hate to be 'that guy,' " Simon said as he closed the door behind them. "But Miami is three thousand miles away. How are we supposed to get there in time to stop the proposal?"

"We'll fly," Miles said. "My mom gave me an emergency credit card."

"Hello, boys!" crooned Ms. Price from next door. "I'm supposed to be keeping an eye on you."

Miles arched an eyebrow at the Chipmunks. "How are we gonna get to Miami if we've got her watching us?"

"I have a plan," Alvin said.

Simon groaned. "Those are the four words I fear most."

"I can't believe that worked!" Miles said. He and the Chipmunks were standing over a pack of sleeping squirrels.

"It wasn't so much me as it was the peanuts dipped in cough syrup," Alvin told him.

"That's really messed up," Miles said. He nodded slowly. "Respect."

Simon glared at the sleeping squirrels, who were supposed to be standing in for him and his brothers. He seriously doubted Ms. Price was going to be fooled. "Alvin, these aren't even chipmunks. They're squirrels."

Alvin shrugged. "Beggars can't be choosers. Besides, once we put them in the shirts from our Alvin, Simon, and Theodore dolls, Ms. Price won't be able to tell the difference." He nodded to a trio of Beanie Babies sitting on the table.

Simon sighed. "Let's get 'em changed before they wake up."

An hour later, Miles was waiting in line at the airport. He shifted nervously from foot to foot. "I can't believe I maxed out my mom's credit card on one ticket."

Alvin poked his head out of Miles's backpack. "We're fine. Just stick to the plan."

Simon poked his head out of the top of Miles's shirt. "I just want to go on record saying just how much I disagree with *the plan*." He grumbled and burrowed deeper into Miles's shirt as the boy stepped up to the X-ray machine.

Inside Miles's backpack, Alvin held his breath and tried not to move. "What's that?" The security officer pointed to her scanner screen when the backpack went through the X-ray machine.

Miles chuckled. "Oh, uh, it's a stuffed 'Alvin' doll. You know, from that lame singing group of rodents."

Unable to contain his annoyance, Alvin frowned. Then he blinked.

The security officer tilted her head. "I need you to take the doll out of your backpack, please."

Miles was beginning to sweat. This wasn't part of the plan. But as casually as possible, he lifted Alvin out of his backpack. Alvin kept his body stiff as a board, pretending to be a toy.

"See?" Miles said, holding Alvin up. He moved Alvin's arms and legs like a stuffed animal. "It bends, it twists . . ." He shoved Alvin's leg up, and it was more than Alvin could take.

"*Owwwww!*" Alvin shrieked.

"It cries!" Miles said loudly, trying to distract the officer. "And this is my favorite part. It even says 'Mommy, I'm scared!' "

Refusing to be humiliated, Alvin remained silent. Miles shook Alvin hard. "I think its battery is low." He whacked Alvin on the back.

Alvin squeaked, "Mommy, I'm scared!"

Miles laughed. But when Alvin chomped his hand, Miles shut up. "Ow! And it bites. Very hard. Design flaw. There was a recall."

The security officer looked at Miles like he was crazy. "Okay, you can put it away now."

Relieved, Miles stuffed Alvin back into his backpack. But then the officer said, "I'll just have you step over here for a quick body search. Put your arms out." The officer began patting Miles down.

Inside Miles's shirt, Simon panicked. He scampered down Miles's shirt and slithered into the leg of his pants instead. "I don't want to go to jail," Simon said, terrified.

The officer was satisfied at last. She shook her head and waved Miles past. "Get out of here."

Miles tossed his backpack over his shoulder and stormed away from the security area. As soon as the coast was clear, he shook Simon out of his pants and stuffed him into the backpack with Alvin. Then he zipped them both in, growling, "You're lucky I don't flush you both down the toilet."

Inside the backpack, Simon looked at Alvin. "I'm glad we packed Theodore in the luggage. He never would have made it through security."

CHAPTER 5

iles, will you ask the flight attendant for peanuts?" Alvin peeked out of the magazine pouch in front of Miles's airplane seat. "We're hungry."

"I'd love a water," Simon said, appearing beside Alvin. "But no ice."

Miles snapped the magazine pouch open, then closed again, sealing the Chipmunks deep inside the pocket. "Shut up and stay out of sight."

Alvin poked his head up. "If you're not going to feed us, then I'm going to forage," he warned Miles.

"That is not a great idea, Alvin," Simon said, his voice muffled inside the magazine pouch. "We're not legitimate passengers!"

But there was no point arguing with Alvin when he had his mind set on something. Before Simon could say *peanuts or pretzels*, Alvin had launched himself out of the magazine pouch. He perched on the headrest in front of Miles's seat and scanned the plane for possible food sources. The man sitting in the seat in front of them saw Alvin and screamed.

"Sorry," Alvin said quietly, to calm the man. "Didn't mean to startle you."

"Oh, no," the man said, holding up his hand. "I don't get startled. It's just . . . you're . . . *you.*"

Alvin grinned. The man recognized him! "Yes! I am me. And if you have a pen, I'm always happy to sign an autograph for a fan."

"Oh, no," the man told him. "I'm definitely not a fan."

"Good talk," Alvin said, and hopped forward. He scampered from row to row through the main cabin but found absolutely nothing worth eating. And the place was packed!

Ahead, he spotted the curtain dividing the main cabin from first class. First class was more Alvin's speed. He dashed up the aisle and slipped under the curtain.

"Ahhhh . . ." Alvin said, tucking himself into an open seat. He grabbed a steaming plate of pasta off the service cart and dug in. But he stopped shoveling the tasty noodles into his mouth when he noticed his neighbor giving him a funny look. "What? You've never seen a Chipmunk in first class before?"

The guy lifted his chin. "Actually, I recently flew next to the Chipettes, and they were ladies."

"Are you saying I'm an animal?" asked Alvin, devouring more of his food.

"No." The guy shook his head. "That would be offensive to animals."

"Excuse me," a flight attendant said, stopping beside Alvin's seat. "Can I help you?"

Alvin nodded politely. "Yes. Would you be a doll and get me a sparkling water? I'd love to cleanse my palate before diving into the cheese plate." He burped. Loudly. "Scratch that. Palate cleansed!"

The flight attendant narrowed her eyes. "May I see your boarding pass?"

Alvin knew he was busted. He put on his most charming smile—and then took off.

*   *   *

Meanwhile, in the underbelly of the plane, Theodore wasn't exactly having the ride of his life. He was uncomfortable, and it was freezing inside the luggage compartment. He looked around at some of the other animals riding alongside him. "Hi, everyone. Cold in here, isn't it?"

The other animals glanced up at him with sad eyes but said nothing.

"Tough crowd." He peeked over at a parrot that kept staring at him. "You seem nice."

The parrot repeated, "You seem nice."

"Oh, thank you," Theodore said happily.

"Thank you," the parrot said.

"You're welcome," Theodore told him.

"You're welcome," the parrot echoed.

Theodore strolled over to a few other animals, all of whom were riding in cages. A monkey, jealous of Theodore's freedom, screeched and yelped to get out.

"Shhhh," Theodore warned him. "Inside voices."

The monkey shook the bars of his cage and screamed.

"Stop! You're gonna make the other animals nervous."

The monkey began to cry.

Theodore felt terrible. "Okay, I'll let you out. But you have to promise to behave and go back in your cage before we land."

The monkey nodded, so Theodore let him out. This set off a chorus of whining from all the other animals.

Now Theodore felt *really* terrible. The next thing he knew, he was unlocking all the cages.

As the animals swarmed around him, clamoring and crying, Theodore had a sinking feeling he'd made a big mistake.

*　　*　　*

Back in the main cabin, Alvin was scampering around as fast as he could. The flight attendant was angry. Alvin wondered if he'd accidentally stolen *her* plate of pasta. Oh, well. Finders keepers. "Run!" he ordered Simon. "Hide!"

Simon threw his hands up. "Where? We're on a plane!"

They both dodged and weaved through the airplane, leaving a path of destruction in their wake.

"Everybody freeze!" The guy who had recognized Alvin earlier in the flight stood up and held a badge in the air. "I'm Agent Suggs, air marshal!"

Everyone on board froze. Everyone, that is, except a parade of animals who'd just burst out of the luggage compartment. A monkey, a pack of dogs, several cats, and a parrot burst into the airplane's main cabin . . . followed by Theodore.

"Oh, this can't be good," Alvin said, still not moving a muscle.

"Theodore," Simon said, "what happened?!"

"Please don't blame us. Cargo is a cold and horrible place," Theodore told his brothers.

The plane lurched. Everyone toppled over as oxygen masks fell from overhead.

A bell rang. "Um, I think that sound means we're supposed to return to our seats?" Alvin said.

Agent Suggs lunged for Alvin. But Alvin grabbed an oxygen mask and swung through the cabin.

"I said don't move!" the air marshal boomed as he dove for Alvin again.

"This is your captain speaking," a calm voice spoke through the intercom system. "We apologize for the turbulence, but we were momentarily distracted by a parrot in the cockpit. Everything is under control, but we will be making an emergency landing in Austin, Texas."

"You heard him!" Agent Suggs announced to the plane's passengers. "Plane's going down!"

Everyone screamed.

"No, no, not down, like . . . down, down. Safely down. We are not crashing," Agent Suggs clarified.

"Great speech," Alvin muttered as the passengers continued to scream in terror.

"Hey!" Agent Suggs shouted. "You watch who you're taking to. I'm the police of the sky!" The parrot swooped through the cabin, leaving behind a big dropping on the air marshal's shirt.

"You're welcome," the parrot chirped.

Theodore giggled. "Such a polite bird."

Agent Suggs roared, "That's it!" He grabbed at Alvin. This time, he caught him. "Enough is enough! I've had it with Chipmunks on this plane!"

* * *

Once the plane had safely landed at the Austin airport, Agent Suggs dragged the three Chipmunks and Miles to the security office and began grilling them about what had happened. "Okay, so just to make sure we have everything . . . you released animals from the cargo area and then forced an emergency landing?"

"We also snuck onto the plane," Theodore confessed.

"Theodore!" Simon yelped.

"He said 'everything.'" Theodore shrugged.

"That's three major incidents on one flight," said Agent Suggs. "Which is three more incidents than I've had in all my years as an air marshal."

"Congratulations on such a distinguished career, sir," said Miles.

"Distinguished," Suggs grunted. "That's right. And because of that career, I have a meeting with Homeland Security next week about a promotion."

"Another congratulations, sir," Miles said.

"But now my career is blemished, because of you. You blemished it," Agent Suggs snarled.

Simon cocked his head. "It's such a tiny blemish. More like a freckle."

"Really?" Agent Suggs asked. "What do you think they'll remember when I go for my interview? My decade of perfect service? Or the one time three chipmunks turned my flight into a zoo?"

"Probably the time with the chipmunks," Theodore squeaked.

Alvin nudged him.

"Sorry, I'm not good at this," Theodore said.

"Look," said Alvin. "We feel terrible about what happened. And the only reason we snuck onto the flight was to deal with a family emergency."

"And if you check," Simon went on, "we also have a clean travel record. We've flown thousands of miles without incident. See, we're musicians—"

Alvin cut him off. "He knows who we are. Not a fan."

"No, I am not," Agent Suggs snapped.

"Sir, what could we have possibly done to make you hate us so much?" Simon asked.

Agent Suggs sighed sadly. "I'll tell you what you did. It was last Christmas Eve. My girlfriend, Anna, came over to exchange gifts. It was our first Christmas together, and I wanted it to be perfect . . ."

The Chipmunks and Miles all exchanged awkward glances as Agent Suggs told them about how he'd been planning to ask Anna to marry him, but instead, she'd broken up with him. Now his life was ruined . . . all because he had proposed to Anna with one of the Chipmunks' biggest hits playing in the background.

"She broke up with me because of your song. Because of you," Agent Suggs said accusingly.

Alvin, Simon, Theodore, and Miles gave one another a look that said they were all pretty sure Agent Suggs was nuttier than a salted nut roll.

"But now," Agent Suggs went on. "It's payback time. You three are on the No Fly List."

"What?!" The Chipmunks gasped. "No! You can't do that."

Agent Suggs beamed. "I just did. And not only that, I'm going to hold you three in custody until my interview, and then walk you into Homeland Security as an example of what I do to criminals."

"*Criminals* sounds like such a *strong* word," Simon said.

"Strong like the tiny bars I'm gonna lock you behind." Suggs laughed. "You messed with the wrong person when you ruined my relationship. I'm an air marshal. All powerful. All seeing. All knowing."

"Then you obviously know you just made that entire speech with your tie in a cup of coffee, right?" Alvin said, nodding down at the table.

Agent Suggs glanced down. He jumped up and started storming out of the room. "I'll be back in two minutes."

Alvin yelled after him, "You also still have a little parrot dropping on your shoulder."

"I'll be back in ten minutes," Suggs said. He marched back to the table and leaned toward the Chipmunks. "And don't even think about leaving. Because I have a very particular set of skills. Skills I have acquired over a very long career. Skills that make me a nightmare for chipmunks like you."

Alvin glanced down at Agent Suggs's hand. "Um, you just put your hand on an ink pad."

Suggs looked down. His hand was, in fact, covered in ink. "Fifteen minutes. I'll be back."

The minute the door closed behind Agent Suggs, Alvin leaped up. "That guy is the mayor of Crazytown. Let's get outta here."

"Alvin's right," said Miles. "He's got it in for you guys, no matter what. We can't make it any worse than it is."

Alvin rifled around in a drawer and pulled out a tube of superglue. "I think we got off on the wrong foot with Agent Suggs. Time for a little bonding."

CHAPTER 6

Alvin, Simon, Theodore, and Miles were long gone when Agent Suggs returned to his office. Now that he was in a clean shirt and tie, he felt a lot more confident. He flung open the door, ready to put the Chipmunks in their place.

"Hello?" he said, staring around the empty room.

55

No one answered.

Agent Suggs was seething. "You messed with the wrong man, Chipmunks. Nobody runs on Agent James Suggs."

Through the window on the far side of his office, there was a flash of movement. Suggs spotted the Chipmunks and Miles—they were making a break for it in a taxi!

He spun around and tried to run after them . . . but his hand was stuck to the doorknob. "Hey!" he screamed. "Stop that cab!"

Suggs pulled on his hand, but it wouldn't budge. "Somebody help! Those Chipmunks glued my hand to the doorknob!"

A minute later, with the doorknob still firmly attached to his hand, Agent Suggs ran through the airport.

"Agent Suggs," he huffed to the guy in charge of the taxi stand. "Air marshal. You just put three Chipmunks and a kid in a taxi. I need to know where it went."

As the cab manager looked through his records, a little kid waiting in line reached out and touched the doorknob attached to Agent Suggs's hand. A few loose screws dangled from the fixture. If he hadn't thought to unscrew the knob, Agent Suggs would have still been stuck to his own office door.

"What's the matter, kid?" Agent Suggs said, annoyed. "You've never seen a guy with a doorknob glued to his hand before?"

Agent Suggs glanced down at the doorknob and steeled his nerves. "Pulling it off. Okay. Quick like a Band-Aid. Here we go. One, two, three . . . *ye-owwww!*"

* * *

While Agent Suggs soothed his hand in a cab, Miles and the Chipmunks plotted their next move.

"This is as far as all my money takes us," Miles said. He asked the cab driver to stop outside a rundown roadhouse in the middle of nowhere.

"That puts us"—Simon pulled up the map app on his phone—"two hours and thirty minutes from Miami."

The others cheered.

Simon held up a hand. "By plane. But since we have no money and no transportation, getting the last thirteen hundred miles should only take us . . . two weeks."

"Two weeks?" Theodore cried.

"Two and a half," Simon said. "I rounded down."

"Ashley's album release party is in three days," said Alvin. "If we're gonna have any shot at stopping this proposal, we need to get to Miami by then."

Simon's cell phone trilled. He glanced down at the caller ID. "As if we're not in enough trouble already . . . it's Dave."

"Feels like we should let this one go to voice mail," said Alvin.

"But he said he wanted to FaceTime every night at eight, remember?" Theodore told them. "He told us we have to pick up."

"We can't pick up," Miles argued.

"If we don't pick up, Dave will know something is wrong," Simon said.

Miles glared at him. "He's gonna know something is wrong when he sees we're not at home, because we're in *Texas*!"

"So we just have to make him think we *are* at home," Simon said. "All I need is a photo of our house from my phone, and a green screen."

"Oh, a green screen?" asked Miles. "Is that all? I was afraid you were going to need something we couldn't possibly find in a parking lot in the middle of nowhere."

Simon wasn't willing to give up that easily. As Alvin answered the phone, Simon used an old green car in the parking lot as a green screen.

"Hey, guys," Dave said, grinning at them through the phone. "How's it going?"

"Great," Alvin said. "Couldn't be better. Just hanging out around the house."

Dave's coworker Barry stepped into the shot and waved at the Chipmunks. "Is that the Chipmunks? Hi, guys!"

"Hi, Barry!" Alvin, Simon, and Theodore chorused.

Barry squinted into Dave's phone. "Why is your Christmas tree up?"

Simon shrugged. In his haste, the only picture he'd been able to find of their house was from Christmas. Through clenched teeth, he told Alvin, "I grabbed the first photo I could find."

Alvin stammered, "Uh, we, uh—we put it up to get a jump on the holidays!"

"But Christmas is months away," Barry pointed out.

"Yes, it is," Alvin said. "But it always goes by so fast! We just want to make sure we really have time to enjoy it this year, you know?"

Barry nodded, even though he clearly didn't get it. "Well, guys, I gotta run. My girl-friend is here."

As the guys said their good-byes to Barry, a coyote howled.

"What was that?" Dave asked.

"What was what?" Theodore said.

Another howl rang out, louder this time.

"That," said Dave. "It sounded like . . . a coyote?"

"Oh!" Alvin laughed. "That's Miles. We're teaching him how to sing. Right, Miles?"

Miles waved at Dave through the camera. "Yep! I'm a terrible singer. *Woo-ooo!* How's everything going in Miami?"

"Great," said Dave. "Just getting ready for the big event."

Suddenly, a train whistle sounded behind the Chipmunks and Miles.

Dave frowned. "What was *that?*"

"Uh, sorry, Da—" Simon said, making his voice cut out. "Bad connec—"

"Can't hea—" Alvin added. "But we *are* home. Very un-Texas here. Bye!"

In Miami, Dave stared at his phone.

"Everything okay?" Samantha asked.

"No," Dave said. "That was really weird. Even for the boys." He had a feeling it was time to check in with Ms. Price. His call with Alvin, Simon, and Theodore had not left him feeling reassured.

"Oh, hi, Dave!" Ms. Price said when she answered. "I'll peek in on them right now."

Dave waited nervously while Ms. Price went over to check in with the boys.

"Dave?" she said, returning to the phone. Ms. Price had seen a few things in her days, but she'd never seen a house that looked like this. The three little squirrels (Ms. Price had always thought Dave's boys were chipmunks!) in T-shirts were destroying the place! Wood shavings were scattered throughout the house, and couch cushions were torn to shreds. "Dave, they've eaten everything. And I mean *everything*."

Dave chuckled. "That sounds about right. Thanks for checking in on them, Ms. Price." He hung up and smiled at Samantha. "It sounds like they're having a blast."

Miles and the Chipmunks made their way toward the door of the run-down roadhouse.

"Sorry, ramblers," said the owner. "Twenty-one and over."

"But it's almost dark outside and we don't have anywhere else to go," Theodore told him.

The owner shook his head. "I'd love to help you out, boys, but I've got bigger fish to fry. I've got a roadhouse packed with cowboys and bikers, waiting to hear a band whose singer is stuck fifty miles away with a flat tire. So unless you guys know someone who can carry a tune, I'm gonna have to bid you good night."

Alvin, Simon, and Theodore shared a look.

"How would you feel about some singing chipmunks?" asked Alvin.

A few minutes later, the stage was set for the Chipmunks to make their country debut. "Ladies and gentlemen," the owner yelled into the microphone. "Please welcome, all the way from Los Angeles, California . . . the Chipmunks!"

One guy in the audience clapped feebly.

"Thank you!" Theodore said, smiling.

"I wasn't clappin'," said the guy. "I was killing a mosquiter."

With Miles accompanying them on guitar, the Chipmunks began to sing.

As he rocked out in front of the less-than-lively crowd, Alvin beamed at his brothers. "Feels good to be back onstage, doesn't it, guys?"

The Chipmunks felt totally at home in front of a crowd. It was amazing to be performing, even if the audience was less than enthusiastic.

But the good feeling didn't last long. Before they could even wrap their first song, Agent Suggs burst in.

"Alvin," Simon said out of the side of his mouth. "We've got a problem."

"I'm on it," Alvin told the others. "Cover for me."

While his brothers sang on, Alvin leaped off the stage and wound through the line-dancing crowd. Agent Suggs tried to chase him down, but the crowd jostled and pushed him out of the way.

Winking, Alvin peeked out from behind a big biker dude's shaggy beard. "Psst, Suggs! Over here!"

Suggs spun around and lunged for him. "Gotcha!"

But Alvin ducked out of the way, and Suggs found himself with a fistful of the biker's beard instead of a mischievous chipmunk.

Agent Suggs backed away from the biker, who wasn't enjoying his one-on-one time with the air marshal. "Sir, let me explain. I have a reason to believe there is a fugitive chipmunk hiding in your beard."

"You don't think I'd know if there was an animal living in my beard?" the biker snarled.

Alvin popped out from behind the curtain of beard, held out a peanut, and chirped, "Beard peanut?"

Suggs grabbed for Alvin with his other hand. But once again, Alvin slipped out of his grasp.

Now Agent Suggs had *two* hands in the biker's beard, which was two more than the biker was willing to take. He roared and tossed Agent Suggs across the room.

Suggs crashed into a huge cowboy, who snapped at the biker, "Watch where you're throwing people. Some of us are trying to dance."

"What are you gonna do, cowpoke?" the biker sneered.

In a flash, the room full of line dancers became a room full of fighters. Bikers and cowboys tossed one another across the roadhouse, throwing punches and hurling insults.

Simon leaped off the stage, yelling, "I think that's our cue to wrap things up."

"Sorry about the fight," Theodore shouted to the owner.

"No apologies necessary," he said, grinning out at the brawling crowd. "Nothing's better for business than a good old-fashioned brawl. He winked at Simon, Theodore, and Miles as they flew out the door. "Good luck, outlaws."

While his brothers made a hasty escape, Alvin dodged away from Agent Suggs and bolted for the door.

"Outta the way, hillbillies," Suggs said, elbowing his way past a pair of fighters. "I need to get out of this place ASAP!"

The cowboy and the biker, who had been fighting with each other, turned their anger on Suggs. With a grunt, the two guys lifted the air marshal over their heads and tossed him through the front window.

Alvin took the opportunity to zip out the front door.

"Alvin!" Simon hollered from inside a waiting taxi.

Theodore stuck his head out the cab's window. "Come on!"

"Forget about him," Miles told the other two. Alvin was almost there . . . but so was Agent Suggs! "Seriously—just drive, man."

Alvin jumped into the cab as it began to roll away. Suggs ran alongside the cab, grasping for the door handle. Panting, he screamed, "You can't run forever! I'll find you! And when I do, I'll—"

Thwack! Suggs crashed into a pole on the side of the road and fell to the ground. He was out cold.

The Chipmunks cheered. But they didn't get far before they, too, were stopped.

"No money, no ride," the taxi driver announced. "I'm not running an animal shelter. Have a nice night."

The cab driver drove away, leaving Alvin, Simon, Theodore, and Miles stranded by a lone tree in the middle of nowhere.

*   *   *

"I can't sleep without my pillow," Theodore said, tossing and turning to try to find a comfy spot high up in the tree's branches. "I don't suppose they make Tempur-Pedic tree branches, do they?"

"Seriously?" Miles asked. He was propped up against the tree's trunk. "You're the ones who are supposed to be comfortable sleeping in trees, not me."

"We're not talking to you," Alvin said in a huff. "Not after you tried to leave me behind back there at the roadhouse."

Miles shrugged. "First—awesome, because I don't want to talk to you. Second—you guys would have done the same thing to me."

"No," Alvin said. "We would have waited for you."

Theodore nodded. "Yeah, we're in this together. You mess with one of us—"

Miles cut him off. "I've heard your lame family motto. But I don't believe it, man. People look out for themselves. It's biology. It's how animals stay alive."

"On behalf of animals, I'd like to say that's incredibly cynical," said Simon.

"Call it whatever you want, dude, it's true," said Miles. "You think my dad was thinking about anyone other than himself when he left my mom?" He shrugged. "He bailed when I was five."

"I'm sorry, Miles," Theodore said.

"Whatever," Miles scoffed. "I don't really care. I've done fine without him."

Quietly, Alvin said, "Just so you know, if Dave and your mom end up together . . . he's a good person. He would never bail on you."

"Then why are you taking this trip?" Miles asked, looking up into the tree. "Oh, that's right.

Because you think he's gonna ditch you. Whatever . . . dads are overrated. Eventually you'll get over him leaving you."

"Really?" asked Simon, feeling sad. He didn't want to think about Dave leaving them. He loved Dave, and it would hurt to lose his dad.

"Yeah," Miles said. He closed his eyes.

Lost in their own thoughts, all four guys drifted off to sleep.

When morning came, it was time to get back on the road again. Miles and the Chipmunks set off, hoping they wouldn't be too late to stop Dave's proposal.

"I can't . . ." Theodore said, after they'd been walking for what felt like forever. "I'm too tired."

"Dude," Miles said, glancing over his shoulder. "Are you joking? I can still see the tree we slept in." He kept walking. "It's ten miles to the bus station. Can't you guys walk any faster?"

"Uh, given that our legs are ninety percent shorter than yours, we're actually walking fifty-eight percent faster than you are, " Simon shot back.

"Nerd alert," Miles muttered. Glancing at Simon, he could see that he'd hurt his feelings. Reluctantly, he patted his shoulder and bent down. "Fine, come on up."

The Chipmunks hopped onto his shoulder and got comfy.

"This is actually quite an efficient way to travel," Simon said.

Alvin giggled. "I could go for miles on Miles."

For the next few hours, the Chipmunks relaxed while Miles trudged the ten miles to the bus stop. There they bought a ticket to New Orleans and hopped on the next bus. When the bus pulled into New Orleans, Miles looked at the Chipmunks and said, "Only eight hundred and sixty-three miles to go."

Though they were a little closer to Miami than they had been a few hours before, the Chipmunks were worried they'd reached a dead end. They were totally out of money, and there was no way to go any farther unless they made a few bucks.

Luckily, Alvin had a great idea for how to make some cash, fast! Using the streets of New Orleans as their stage, the Chipmunks began to perform. In no time at all, they'd made a decent chunk of change.

Theodore cheered when someone tossed a ten-dollar bill in front of them. "Ten dollars!" he said. "Looks like our luck is turning around!"

"Your luck's run out, fellas," said an all-too-familiar voice.

The Chipmunks looked up. Agent Suggs was towering over them. He picked up his ten and smiled smugly.

"How'd you find us?" asked Simon.

"I'm an air marshal. Law enforcement is my life. All I need is my wits, my badge, and my gun," Suggs replied.

"They let *you* carry a gun?" Miles asked.

"No," Agent Suggs said quietly. "A stun gun, though." He tapped the weapon strapped to his thigh. "Now, we can either do this the easy way, or the hard way."

"My brothers and I would like to discuss our options," Alvin told him. He pulled the others aside and whispered, "Slingshot, on three . . . One, two—"

Agent Suggs put his hands on his hips. "Let's go. I don't have all day."

"Three!" Alvin yelled.

Simon and Theodore each lifted one of Alvin's legs and set him flying like a missile at Agent Suggs.

Pow! Alvin crashed into Suggs's midsection. The agent doubled over in pain.

Alvin popped up. "Spoiler alert, Suggs. We chose the hard way."

Miles and the Chipmunks ran. But this time, Suggs wasn't down for long. He brushed himself off and chased after them.

Alvin, Simon, Theodore, and Miles raced through the crowded streets, dodging and weaving around groups of late-night partiers.

"Guys!" Theodore screeched. "He's on my tail!"

"You can lose him, Theodore," Alvin told his brother.

"No," Theodore said. "He's literally *on* my tail."

Alvin and Simon slid to a stop. They looked back and saw that Suggs had his meaty foot pressed down on top of Theodore's tail.

"Where you going, little fella?" Suggs said, taunting Theodore. "Spoiler alert: You're going to chipmunk jail." He picked up Theodore and dangled him in front of his face. "With tiny bars and a tiny barbed-wire fence, and a tiny toi-let and a tiny yard where you can work out with tiny little weights."

Theodore considered Suggs's threat. "That actually sounds adorable."

Alvin ran at Agent Suggs, scrambling up the big man's leg. He grabbed for Suggs's stun gun.

"Hey, what does this do?" Alvin pulled the trigger, releasing a blast into Suggs's leg.

"Don't tase me, bro!" Suggs said. He reached down for his wounded leg. As he did, Simon grabbed Theodore and they all dashed away again. Suggs hobbled after them.

When they reached an arcade, Miles and the Chipmunks ducked inside. The Whac-A-Mole game was the perfect place for three chipmunks to hide out! They burrowed down into the holes, hidden from view.

But Suggs was onto them. "You gotta come out sometime," he said, holding the big mallet over the board.

Alvin popped out and stuck out his tongue. "If you insist!"

Suggs swung the mallet at him, but Alvin ducked back into the hole just before it hit him.

"Over here," Simon said, poking his head up.

"No, over here," Theodore said. Suggs swung wildly at the board, trying to hit each of the chipmunks as they popped into view.

Eager to help, Miles peeked over Suggs's shoulder and called out, "No, up here!"

Once again, Suggs swung the mallet—and whacked himself in the face!

"Nice one, Miles!" cheered Alvin.

While Suggs recovered, the Chipmunks burst back out onto the street.

"I think we lost him," Miles panted.

"Don't move!" Agent Suggs boomed from behind him.

"Oh, good," Alvin grumbled. "We found him."

They raced across the street and stepped right into the middle of a wild parade. "Hey! Over here!" Simon called, waving at Agent Suggs from the top of a trumpet.

Suggs reached for him but took a trumpet blast to the face instead.

"Hi there!" Theodore called out from on top of a tuba.

The agent staggered toward Theodore.

Boooooom! The tuba blasted him out of the way.

"Okay, you got me," Alvin said, waving

to Suggs from the slide of a trombone. "I give up!"

Suggs lunged for Alvin, but the trombone—and Alvin—slid out of his grasp. Suggs stumbled, and a moment later, the trombone's slide shot forward and whacked him in the face. Suggs hit the ground, out cold.

Miles and the Chipmunks high-fived one another.

As the parade raged on, the Chipmunks decided to celebrate by joining the fun. So they climbed up onto one of the floats and rocked out with the band.

In Miami, Dave and Samantha were enjoying a lovely evening in the hotel restaurant.

"This whole day has been incredible," Samantha said, smiling.

Dave held her hand. "It's been the perfect day."

Suddenly, something on the restaurant's TV caught his eye. Dave's eyes widened as he watched the news. "Coming up . . . the Chipmunks are back!" the announcer was saying.

"What?" Dave gasped. He could feel himself beginning to sweat.

The announcer smiled. "You heard me. The Chipmunks are making some noise in New Orleans tonight!"

"Oh, no . . ." Samantha muttered. The broadcast switched over to a shot of the Chipmunks and Miles, dancing and singing on top of a parade float.

"Hey, Alvin," a reporter said, stretching a microphone out to interview Alvin. "Is this a surprise performance announcing the Chipmunks' comeback?"

"Don't call it a comeback . . . 'cause we never left!" Alvin yelled into the mic. He waved at the crowds of people. "I say *party!* You say—"

"Al-viiiiiiin!" Dave screamed.

The next morning, Agent Suggs woke up feeling like he'd been hit by a ton of bricks . . . or, perhaps, the slide of a trombone. He curled into a ball and touched his throbbing head. Gingerly, he eased one eye open. The floor around him was littered with instruments, overturned furniture, and piles of trash.

"What happened last night?" he asked aloud.

Someone leaned over him and grinned. Suggs jumped up and screamed. "Aghhh!"

The man backed away. "Jimmy! Relax, man, it's Vito!"

Suggs stared back at the guy, confused.

"From the band. You don't remember?" Vito asked.

"I remember getting hit in the face with a trombone," Agent Suggs said, cringing. "But that's all."

"That makes sense," Vito said. "I think you had a pretty nasty concussion."

Agent Suggs frowned. "You let me sleep with a concussion?"

"We tried to take you to the hospital," Vito said with a shrug. "But you wouldn't let us. So we all hit a bunch of jazz clubs . . ."

"We?" Suggs asked, confused.

"You, me, your Chipmunk friends . . ."

"I was with the Chipmunks?"

"All night," Vito nodded.

Suggs screamed. This time, the Chipmunks were *really* going to get it.

Meanwhile, Miles and the Chipmunks were waiting in the baggage claim section of the New Orleans airport.

"This is where they told us to meet them, right?" Alvin asked.

Miles nodded. "Hopefully they had time to cool off on the plane."

From across the room, the Chipmunks heard Dave's voice call, "There you are!"

"Dave!" they all yelled together.

"Mom!" shouted Miles.

Dave stomped toward them. "Don't you 'Dave, Mom' us!"

Samantha pulled Dave aside. "You know what, Dave? You're an artist, you're emotional, you follow your heart. I love that, but maybe I should take the lead on this one? Keep a level head. Give 'em a little 'good cop,' you know?"

Dave nodded.

Samantha turned to the guys, took a deep breath, and screamed, "Don't you 'Dave, Mom' us! Do you have any idea how terrifying it is to find out your kids are two thousand miles away from where they're supposed to be? You're lucky there are witnesses, because I'm so mad right now I could—"

Dave pulled her back. "Okay, okay . . . nice work, good cop."

Alvin stepped forward. "Dave, I swear, it wasn't as crazy as it looked on TV."

"Really?" Dave said, eyes narrowed. "Let me just read a few of Theodore's tweets from last night. 'Craziest night ever. I heart New Orleans!' Or, 'In a New Orleans jazz parade! So crazy!' Or, 'If you want to get crazy, go to New Orleans! It's the craziest!'"

"We're sorry, Dave," said Simon, hanging his head.

"Sorry's not gonna cut it this time," Dave said. "If it were up to me, I'd take you guys home right now. But I have to be in Miami for Ashley's record release party tomorrow night."

Slow smiles spread across the Chipmunks' faces.

"Do not smile!" warned Dave. "You three are grounded in Miami. And also when we get back to LA."

"When are we *not* grounded?" Alvin asked.

"You will be so old your fur will be gray," Dave promised.

"That goes for your fur, too, Miles," Samantha said.

"I don't have fur," Miles reminded her.

"Fur, hair, whatever. You're grounded for a long time. Let's go." Samantha stormed off, with the others trailing along after her.

Alvin nudged Miles. "They didn't kill us after all."

Miles smiled at him. "Feels like a win."

"Operation: No Proposal is still on!" Alvin held up his fist, and Miles bumped it.

When they reached the ticket counter, Samantha stopped and looked at Dave. "Are you sure about this?" she asked him. "Because if our three-ring circus is too scary for you, I totally get it. Miles and I can just head back to LA. You wouldn't be the first guy to head for the hills when we showed our crazy cards."

"Please," Dave said, laying a hand on her arm. "Your circus only has one ring. Mine is the three-ringer. My crazy cards will always beat your crazy cards. You're the one who should think about heading for the hills. But if not, I'd still love for you to be my date to the party."

Samantha grinned at him. "I'd love it."

"Great," said Dave. "We'll meet you at the gate."

Samantha and Miles bought their tickets and made their way to the departure gate.

Dave and the Chipmunks stepped up to the ticket counter. "Two more tickets on that same flight, please." He gestured to the Chipmunks and added, "They share a seat."

The ticket agent looked at her computer monitor, and then back at the Chipmunks.

"Is there a problem?" Dave asked.

"There sure is," said the agent. She spun her monitor around.

A picture of the Chipmunks filled the screen, along with the words NO FLY LIST.

*   *   *

"At least we're not on the No Drive List," Theodore said sheepishly. He and his brothers were strapped into the front seat of a rental car together, with a furious Dave in the driver's seat beside them.

"There's no such thing as a No Drive List, Theodore," muttered Simon.

"I'm sure you guys will find a way to start one," said Dave.

"Let's not overreact, Dave," Alvin said. "There's tons of stuff on the No Fly List: fireworks, knitting needles, babies—"

"Babies aren't on the No Fly List," said Simon.

Alvin sighed. "All right, well, the point is, the only reason we left home in the first place—"

"Not now!" Dave yelled, thumping his hand on the steering wheel. "I have worked my butt off on Ashley's album and now, because of you guys, I might not even be there for the release.

Not to mention, you've ruined the trip for me and Samantha."

The Chipmunks gave each other low fives, out of Dave's line of sight.

"I'm way too upset for anything good to come out of this conversation," Dave added.

"It's just . . ." Theodore began. "When you took Samantha to Miami and left us behind—"

Dave thumped the wheel again. "What did I just say, Theodore? I'm not in the mood to hear it! I honestly don't know what to do with you guys anymore."

Alvin opened his mouth to say something, but Simon stopped him. "Don't. You'll just make it worse. Keep pushing him and he might figure out that what he really wants is to leave us behind."

Theodore hung his head.

For once, the Chipmunks were silent. Simon might be right, and none of them wanted to consider what life would be like without Dave.

Back in New Orleans, Agent Suggs was finally well enough to get back on his Chipmunk hunt. He stepped up to the counter at the rental car office. "Agent Suggs, air marshal. Did three chipmunks try to rent a car?"

"Uh," said the employee, "what did they look like?"

"How many chipmunks tried to rent cars from you today?" Agent Suggs blurted.

The employee nodded slowly. "Um, were they like, this tall, and brown, and furry—"

"You're describing a chipmunk, yes," Suggs barked.

"Yeah," said the rental car agent. "They were with some guy. Probably their dad."

Agent Suggs shook his head. "Probably not, because he was a human and they were chipmunks."

"Families come in all shapes and sizes, sir. It's not for me to judge," the rental car agent said.

"I need the information for the GPS unit in that rental car," Suggs replied.

"Oh, we don't track our vehicles," said the rental car employee.

"Listen to me, kid," Suggs growled in his most commanding voice. "I work for the government.

I know what gets tracked. And rental cars definitely get tracked. So go back there and get me the GPS info for that car."

The agent nodded and hopped off her stool.

"Oh, and one more thing. I need to run these fugitives down, so in the name of Uncle Sam, I'm gonna need the fastest car you've got."

The car rental employee disappeared, returning a few minutes later with keys to Suggs's vehicle. Together they headed into the parking lot and checked out Agent Suggs's new ride.

"Are you kidding me?" he said, gaping at the tiny, sad-looking car. "I can't drive this. It looks like a roller skate with wheels."

"Don't roller skates *have* wheels?" asked the car rental employee.

"I'm law enforcement," Suggs reminded her. "I need something more intimidating. I've had dogs bigger than this. It looks like a toaster."

The rental car employee tsked at Agent Suggs. "This car didn't do anything to you, sir, so I don't see a need to insult it. And we're pretty low on inventory, so it's all we have. Here's the GPS info you asked for."

Scowling, Suggs crawled into the car and switched on the tracking device. "Those rodents have a hundred-and-twenty-mile head start. Time to roll up some road."

Up ahead, Dave and the Chipmunks were making great progress on their road trip. Though the drive was long and boring, Dave let them stop and stretch their legs every once in a while.

When Dave was busy filling their tank with gas in Alabama, each of the Chipmunks stocked up on necessities: snacks (Simon and Theodore), and a few cool fireworks (Alvin). The group was nearing Florida when Dave stopped for a quick break in a parking lot right beside a restaurant and arcade.

Theodore begged Dave to go in.

"Easy, Theodore," said Dave. "We're just making a pit stop and then we're getting back on the road."

But when he looked at his kids, he could see they were all desperate to go in and play. Since they were making such good time, Dave reluctantly agreed.

"Thanks, Dave," said Theodore, digging into a piece of pizza a few minutes later. "I just needed a little snack to get me from lunch to dinner."

Alvin ran over to them, waving something in the air. "Look what I won!"

It was an Alvin doll. Even Dave cracked up a little, seeing Alvin holding a stuffed version of himself.

An hour later, the guys were back in the car again. Little did they know that their pizza stop had given Agent Suggs just enough time to catch up to them. The air marshal's tiny car pulled up alongside them, and Agent Suggs honked to try to get their attention. He waved his arms around like crazy.

Dave waved back less enthusiastically.

"What's going on, Dave?" Alvin asked, noticing Dave's glances out the car window.

"Some wacko in the next lane," Dave said, trying to ignore Agent Suggs.

The Chipmunks peeked up over the edge of the window. They spotted Suggs at the exact same moment he spotted them. The air marshal started mouthing threats at the Chipmunks, and all three of them dropped back out of sight.

"What are we gonna do?" Simon whispered urgently.

"This has gotten way out of control," Alvin said. "We have to talk to him."

Simon nodded. "Great idea. One tiny thing, though: He's in a moving vehicle. One more tiny thing: So are we. Also, he's insane."

"We're in enough trouble with Dave already," Alvin said. "The last thing he needs to find out is that a cop is after us. Time for Operation: Fast and Furriest!"

"I don't love that," Simon said, shaking his head. "What about Fast and Squirreliest?"

"Guys," Theodore squeaked, "maybe we can just do the mission without a name?"

Alvin and Simon nodded.

"Gear check," said Simon.

The Chipmunks all dumped out their food bags from the gas station. "Bubble gum, a Tic Tac, an empty bag of licorice, an empty box of cookies . . . Theodore, how much did you eat?!"

Theodore burped.

Simon rolled his eyes and picked up the Tic

Tac. "It'll have to do. Maybe we can bribe him with the Tic Tac?"

"We also have these . . ." Alvin said, pulling out the fireworks he had purchased during their gas stop.

"Fireworks?" Simon asked. "Alvin, Dave is going to freak when he finds out!"

"I'm sorry!" Alvin said. "They were on sale! And you know I can't resist pyrotechnics. I love fireworks like Pharrell loves weird hats and LeBron loves headbands and—"

Simon cut him off. "Alvin, this is a diplomatic mission!"

"I totally agree," Alvin said, nodding. "We're just bringing them as a deterrent. Like you said, this guy is nuts."

Simon considered this for a moment. At last, he said, "Fine. But *only* as a deterrent."

A moment later, they were both ready for the mission-without-a-name. Alvin and Simon chomped sticks of gum as they filled their back-packs with fireworks.

"Theodore," Alvin instructed, "you keep Dave occupied."

"Uh . . ." Theodore glanced up into the front seat. "Okay, um . . . hey, Dave, can I tell you about the dream I had?"

"Sure, Theodore," Dave said.

While Theodore kept Dave busy, Alvin and Simon stuck their wads of chewed-up gum to their hands and feet.

"Let's do this!" Alvin said. He rolled down the window, yelling up to Dave, "Just getting a little fresh air!"

Then, quietly and quickly, Alvin and Simon leaped out the window of Dave's car and landed—*splat!*—on the back windshield of Agent Suggs's vehicle. The gum helped them cling to the car even as it careened down the highway.

Lifting one paw at a time, Alvin and Simon made their way around the side of the car until Alvin opened the back door. He and Simon slipped into the backseat and slammed the door closed again.

Agent Suggs glanced into the rearview mirror. He did a double take when he realized he had guests.

"Hello," Alvin said, waving at him.

"What are you doing in my car?!" Suggs screamed.

"Okay," Alvin said. "First of all, it's not your car, it's obviously a rental. Second of all, we're here to apologize. We even brought you a peace offering." He held out the Tic Tac, and Suggs reluctantly took it from him.

"Tic Tacs are my favorite," Agent Suggs said, considering.

Alvin went on. "Look, we never meant to cause any trouble on the plane, and everything since then—the roadhouse fight, the parade—it's because we're just trying to stop our dad from getting engaged."

"Oh," Agent Suggs said. "Well, why didn't you say so? In that case I accept your—" He broke off and dove toward the backseat, trying to surprise Alvin and Simon with his stun gun. "I lied! I hate Tic Tacs!"

Alvin and Simon dove out of the way, accidentally dumping their backpacks in the backseat.

"Fireworks and electricity do not mix well, sir," Simon said as Suggs's stun gun fired a shot right next to the fireworks.

"Si!" Alvin yelled. "Grab the wheel!"

Simon leaped into the front seat and grabbed the wheel. Agent Suggs tried to stun Alvin again, but he ducked out of the way.

"Alvin!" Simon shrieked from the front seat. "I don't know how to drive!"

"It's just like a video game," Alvin told him.

Simon gulped. "Except that we can't start over if we die!"

In the backseat, Agent Suggs kept jabbing at Alvin with the stun gun. "Oh, no . . ." he gasped. He had missed Alvin, but hit the fuse of the fireworks!

"Si," Alvin yelled to his brother. "Out the sunroof!"

The two Chipmunks leaped out of the sunroof and launched themselves at Dave's car just as the fireworks exploded behind them inside Agent Suggs's car.

And I . . . was made of marshmallows, so I ate myself. Then I woke up."

Theodore hastily finished the story of his dream when he saw that Alvin and Simon were climbing into the back window of Dave's rental car.

"That was one crazy dream, Theodore,"

Dave said, shaking his head. He yawned. "These long drives are boring. Do you guys mind if I put on some tunes?" Dave glanced into the rearview mirror. Alvin and Simon were breathing heavily from their mission. But both smiled at him nonchalantly, as though nothing had happened.

Behind them, Agent Suggs's car swerved wildly and then came to a lurching stop on the side of the road. That would keep him off their tails for a while.

The Chipmunks sat back and relaxed. They grinned when they saw the Miami skyline up ahead of them.

"No smiling," Dave said. "You're still grounded, remember?"

When they reached the hotel, Dave led them through a plush lobby and past groups of people relaxing by the pool.

"If this is grounded, ground me for life," Alvin said.

Dave gritted his teeth. "Don't tempt me."

Later that night, after they'd settled in to their hotel room and Dave had ordered them room service for dinner, Alvin felt like it was time to make things right. He hated when Dave was mad at them. "Hey, Dave," he said. "We'd like to do the mature thing and accept partial responsibility for all the trouble we've caused."

"Partial?" Dave raised his eyebrows.

"Sixty-forty on us," Alvin suggested. "Or maybe seventy-thirty?"

Dave straightened his tie, checking himself in the mirror. "Look, as much as I hate the idea of letting you three out of my sight for even a second, Samantha and I have dinner plans I can't get out of. So if anything happens while I'm gone, we're at Casa Mandolina in Little Havana."

"Ooh," Theodore said. "Romantic."

There was a knock at the door. Dave swung it open, and Samantha and Miles came in.

Samantha gave Miles a pointed look. "You do not leave this room, young man. Understood?"

Alvin waved her off. "You guys don't have to worry about us. We've put you through enough. We'll be on our best behavior tonight."

"I'd love to take your word on that," Dave said. "But I'd be the world's dumbest father if I did. A babysitter is on her way up. She'll be here soon. We'll be home after the party."

Samantha headed out the door, but Dave turned back at the last minute. "Wow, I almost forgot . . ." He reached into his bag and pulled out the ring box! He slipped it into his pocket. "See you guys later."

The door closed.

"Dave's going to propose tonight!" Simon cried.

Miles rolled his eyes. "How could you tell? Because he took an engagement ring to a romantic dinner with his girlfriend?"

"Alvin," Simon yowled, "what are we going to do?"

"Nothing," Alvin said, relaxing on the bed.

"I'm with Alvin," Miles said. "If they're happy, we should be happy for them."

"Nothing?!" Simon said. "Alvin, *nothing* isn't a plan! We can't do *nothing*!"

"Sure we can." Alvin shrugged. "Good luck proposing without this . . ." He held up his hand and smirked. He had the ring!

"We did it?" Theodore asked.

"We did it," Alvin said.

"We did it!" Simon said. The Chipmunks bounced on the beds, cheering.

Miles watched sadly as the Chipmunks celebrated. Then he turned and slipped out of the room.

"Come on, Miles," Alvin called after him. "Join the party!"

But Miles was gone.

In a flash, the Chipmunks were after him. They chased him out of the hotel.

"Come on, Miles," Alvin called. "Let's celebrate. We did it."

Miles hung his head. "Yeah, you got Dave back and we're not gonna be brothers," he muttered. "Mission accomplished. So we don't have to hang out with one other anymore."

"Look, Miles," Alvin said. "Just because we're not going to be brothers doesn't mean we can't be friends."

"Yeah," Simon added. "I thought we had a fun time in New Orleans."

Miles shrugged. "So did I. And then the

second you guys found out we weren't going to be related, you celebrated like you won the Super Bowl. So . . . see ya." Miles slipped his earbuds in and started crossing the street.

Alvin, Simon, and Theodore looked at one another, ashamed. Then, suddenly, Alvin spotted a car driving too fast. It was headed straight for Miles.

"Miles!" he screamed.

"He's wearing earbuds," Simon said. "He can't hear you!"

"Slingshot on three," Theodore said. "One, two, THREE!"

Alvin and Simon fired Theodore right at Miles. He hit Miles square in the back, knocking him forward to safety. Brakes squealed, and the car veered to the side—hitting Theodore and sending him flying!

"Theodore!" Alvin yelled. He and Simon ran to their brother's side.

Miles spun around, realizing what had happened. "Theodore! Is he okay?"

Theodore lay there limply. But finally, his eyes fluttered open.

"I smell empanadas," he whispered. "Is this heaven?"

Simon laughed. "No, it's South Beach."

He and Alvin wrapped Theodore in a huge hug.

"Theodore, you saved my life," Miles said gratefully.

"You mess with one of us . . ." Theodore began, nodding to Miles.

Miles shook his head. "Dude, don't make me say it. It's so lame."

Alvin cocked his head. "He got hit by a car for you, Miles."

Miles closed his eyes and sighed. "You mess with one of us . . . you mess with all of us." He opened his eyes and smiled.

"We're sorry, Miles," Alvin said. "We haven't been fair to you from day one. And the truth is, after spending some time with you . . . you wouldn't be the worst brother."

"I feel the same about you guys," Miles said.

"Can a Chipmunk get a hug?" Theodore asked.

"So I guess we're gonna be family after all," Alvin said.

"Except for one tiny detail," Simon said. "By stealing the ring, we've effectively ruined the proposal."

Alvin leaped up. "We need to get the ring and get to the restaurant!"

"Their reservation was at seven," Alvin said, hustling through the hotel lobby a few minutes later. "We still might have time to save the proposal."

"Uh-oh," Simon said, pointing across the lobby. It was Agent Suggs!

Alvin handed the ring to Miles just as Agent Suggs spotted them. "Just get the ring to Dave," he said.

"I'm not leaving you guys," Miles said.

"He's after us," Alvin said. "This is the only way we can pull this off. Go!"

Miles ran out of the lobby as the Chipmunks dashed through the hotel. Agent Suggs raced after them.

Alvin led his brothers into the elevator and pushed the button for the top floor. As the doors were about to close, a meaty arm reached inside the elevator and forced them open again.

"Gotcha!" Agent Suggs said proudly. He stepped into the elevator and let the doors close. "Enjoy the ride, boys. It's the last one you'll ever take as free chipmunks."

Behind him, Alvin gave his brothers a sign. Theodore and Simon scurried up the wall of the elevator while Suggs gloated. "I'll turn you over to Homeland Security and they'll put you in some kind of zoo prison for dangerous animals, I assume. Ooh! Or maybe I'll have you stuffed! Did you really think you could destroy my rental car, on which, by the way, I did not purchase supplemental insurance?"

Boom!

Alvin pressed the EMERGENCY STOP button and Suggs lost his balance, landing on the elevator floor.

"What are you doing?" Suggs barked. He looked up just in time to see Simon and Theodore scurrying up and out the top of the elevator.

"Trapping you in the elevator," Alvin explained as he raced up the wall to join his brothers. He waved at Agent Suggs.

"Get back here!" Suggs cried, grabbing at him.

But the Chipmunks were too far out of reach. Up above Suggs's head, Simon fiddled with the elevator's fuse box. He scanned the switches, then flipped one. "And . . . elevator power off."

Suggs pressed a button inside the elevator, but it wasn't going anywhere. "No! No, no, no . . ."

Alvin peeked through the hole in the ceiling and called down, "Also, *you* lit the fireworks with your stun gun, so it kinda feels like the rental car is on you. Have a nice night!"

Alvin, Simon, and Theodore raced out of the hotel, desperately trying to catch up to Miles. When the three brothers arrived at the restaurant, out of breath, they found Miles peering in the front window.

Miles grinned and high-fived the Chipmunks. "What happened to Officer Smiley?"

"His elevator got stuck," Simon said.

"Has Dave proposed yet?" Alvin asked.

Miles shook his head. "No, but they're on dessert, so it can't be long. Let's go."

Inside the restaurant, Miles and the Chipmunks hid behind a plant. They watched Dave step away from his table and give something to the maître d'.

"That's the box!" Simon whispered.

As soon as Dave made his way back to his table, Alvin nudged the others. "It's go time!" He popped out from behind the plant, but before he could make a break for Dave's table, the maître d' stopped them.

"Excuse me," he said, holding up a hand.

"But if you gentlemen don't have a reservation, I'm going to have to ask you to leave."

Alvin zipped through his legs. As the maître d' chased after him, Alvin zoomed through the restaurant, winding his way between the tables to Dave and Samantha. "I'm open!" he called to Miles.

Miles threw the ring as high and far as he could. It went sailing through the air. Alvin sprinted after it, knowing this was the most important catch of his life.

But unless there was some sort of miracle, he wouldn't make it. The ring was flying too fast and too far. Alvin jumped up—and landed inside a bucket of ice, next to a bottle of champagne.

Thinking fast, Alvin leaped onto the bottle just as a waiter picked it up and uncorked it. The cork flew out of the bottle . . . and so did Alvin! He rode the cork across the room and landed with a *splat* right in the middle of Dave's table. He reached his hand out for the ring . . . and caught it!

"Hi, Dave," he said, holding the ring up like a prize.

Dave's face turned bright red. It looked like he was about to explode.

"Don't say it," Alvin said quickly. "We all know you want to say it, and no one would judge you for saying it, but hear me out."

Miles, Simon, and Theodore made their way across the room to join them. Samantha looked from Alvin to Miles. "Miles! What . . . ? That's it. I'm sending you to one of those camps where they kidnap you out of your bed in the middle of the night." She paused, and then added, "Maybe."

"Mom, please," Miles begged. "Just let us explain."

Alvin broke in. "We came to Miami to stop you two from getting engaged."

Samantha looked from Alvin to Dave, clearly surprised.

Alvin cringed. "And I just blew the surprise. That one's on me. *But!* This is the part I'd like you to focus on: When Theodore got hit by a car—"

"Theodore got hit by a car?" Dave asked.

"He's fine," Alvin said. "He was saving Miles's life; it was very heroic. Anyway, we're getting sidetracked. The point is, we realized we liked the idea of you two being together, and we changed our minds. It might not be the family in the photo that comes with the frame, but it's gonna be our family, and we're proud of it."

Dave cleared his throat. "Guys, that ring isn't mine."

"So . . ." Samantha said, looking at him. "You're not proposing?"

Dave sighed. "I'm sorry, Samantha. I'm not."

"Oh, thank god," said Samantha. "Not that I couldn't see it happening someday, but . . . I want us to take time with this relationship, because I really want it to work."

"Me too," said Dave.

"I'm very confused right now," Alvin said, looking from Dave to Samantha. "You brought this ring to Miami. You said you had to come to dinner."

"The ring is for Barry, my sound engineer. He's proposing to his girlfriend, Alice, at the restaurant tonight," Dave explained.

All six of their heads swiveled around just in time to see Barry get down on one knee in front of a woman. He handed her the box. The *empty* box.

Samantha chewed her lip. "Uh-oh. No woman is going to respond well to an empty ring box."

"It's okay," Alvin said. "It's not empty."

They watched as Barry's girlfriend opened the box.

"A breath mint?!" she shrieked. She slapped Barry across the face and stomped out of the restaurant.

"Alllll-*viiiiin!*" Dave screamed.

ater that night, Alvin was still trying to
apologize to Dave.

"Dave," Alvin said, as he and the
others followed Dave into a fancy nightclub.
"Please let me explain."

Dave led Miles and the Chipmunks into the
club's greenroom, then spun around. "Stop.
The only reason we're not already headed back

to LA is because I have to be here. Samantha and I are going to congratulate Ashley on her album release, and then we're all going home." He shook his head and looked at each of the Chipmunks in turn. "I've never been more disappointed in you guys than I am right now." He stomped back out of the greenroom, leaving Miles and the Chipmunks alone.

"If Dave didn't want to get rid of us before, he definitely does now," Simon said.

"Poor Barry," Theodore said sadly. "He let me eat a couch chip when he wasn't supposed to, and how do I repay him? By ruining his life."

"I wish there was a way we could show him how sorry we are," Simon said.

"I have an idea," Alvin said. He pulled the others into a huddle and explained his plan. They all agreed to try it. After all, it was better than nothing.

"You guys go get Ashley. I'll be right back . . . I'm going to go see some friends who are in Miami," Alvin said.

A little while later, Alvin dashed into the audition room for *American Idol*. The Chipettes were on the judging panel this year, and for this plan to work, Alvin needed all the musical help he could get.

"Alvin!" Eleanor said when he burst into the auditions. "What are you doing here?"

"Yeah! We're in the middle of auditions!" Brittany said.

"I need your help," he told them. "We screwed up with Dave and we need to fix it."

The Chipettes put their heads together. After a moment's discussion, Eleanor nodded. "Because it's for Dave, we're in."

"I won't even ask how badly you guys screwed up this time," Brittany said.

"Thank you," Alvin said. "Because it's pretty bad. Like, *Titanic* bad. Like zombie apocalypse bad. Like—"

"Alvin!" Brittany cut him off. "We said we were in."

Alvin clapped. "Right! Okay, let's go."

He led them back to the nightclub, where Theodore and Simon were still working to convince Ashley to help them with their plan.

"We need your help surprising Dave," Simon pleaded with her.

"Good surprise or bad surprise?" Ashley asked.

Simon grimaced. "Ask us in ten minutes."

Ashley took a deep breath. "Why do I feel like I should walk away from this right now?"

Theodore gave her his most winning smile. "Please don't, Ashley. We really need your help."

Ashley sighed. "Who can resist that face?"

When Alvin and the Chipettes walked into the club, Brittany nodded at Ashley. "They dragged you into this, too?"

"We owe you guys one," Alvin told all the girls. "Okay . . . maybe more than one."

It was time for the show to begin. Everyone in the nightclub was waiting for Ashley to step out and perform her new single. But when she got up onstage, she announced, "I've got a huge surprise for you guys. In fact, it was a surprise to me until just now! Here to perform an original song they just wrote for someone very special to all of us, the producer of this record, David Seville!"

Dave and Samantha both stared up at the stage.

"Please welcome . . . *The Chipmunks*!" Ashley cried.

The stage was flooded with light. The

Chipmunks jumped out onstage and sang the song they had written especially for their favorite dad: Dave.

Samantha squinted at the stage as she recognized the Chipmunks' guitar player. "Miles?"

Miles rocked out behind Alvin, Simon, and Theodore, and Ashley joined in for the chorus.

A record producer in the audience nodded along. "I'm digging this new stuff!"

"I don't know where these guys have been, but I'm glad they're back," another record producer added.

Ashley yelled into the microphone, "Ladies and gentlemen, please welcome the Chipettes!"

The Chipettes raced onstage to join their friends, and everyone in the audience cheered.

Alvin shouted into the mic, "We've got one last surprise. My brothers and I accidentally ruined a very special evening for a very special woman, and we'd like to make it up to her. Alice? Barry has something he'd like to ask you."

A spotlight found Barry and Alice in the audience. With everyone watching, Barry got down on one knee again. This time, he had the real ring in his hand.

Alice nodded and hugged Barry.

Barry gave Alvin, Simon, and Theodore a thumbs-up. "Thanks, Chipmunks!"

Theodore waved. "Thanks for the couch chip, Barry!"

When the Chipmunks'. new song ended, the crowd went wild. Alvin nodded to Brittany. "Thanks, ladies. We owe you one."

Brittany smiled back at him. "You owe us way more than one. But you're welcome."

"We have to get back to auditions now," Jeanette said.

"See you guys back in LA!" Eleanor said.

Out in the crowd, Dave looked around and saw how much the audience loved the boys . . . *his* boys.

As soon as they were offstage, all three Chipmunks ran to him, and Dave scooped them up into a hug.

"We're sorry we came to Miami without telling you," Alvin said.

"We just didn't want to lose you," said Theodore.

"Lose me?" Dave said, incredulous. "Why would you guys ever think you were going to lose me?"

"Because you said you're starting a new chapter in your life," Theodore explained.

"We thought you might bail on us," said Alvin, shrugging.

"Yeah," Simon said. "I mean, technically we're not even a family. We're just three chipmunks who live with you."

Dave shook his head. "Is that what you guys think? Look, I know I haven't been around much lately, and yes, things are changing for us . . . but I would never bail on you, because we are a family. You're stuck with me, whether you like it or not."

The Chipmunks grinned. Samantha and Miles joined them, and Samantha wrapped her arm around Miles.

"Maybe I was a little over the top on the no-music thing," Dave continued. "I still say no tours, but you love to record and perform, so we'll find time for that. Locally." The Chipmunks hugged him even tighter. "And I promise to be a better dad from here on out."

"What are you talking about, Dave?" asked Alvin. "You're the best dad we could ever have."

Dave hugged them again. Then he led his boys, Samantha, and Miles out of the club, onto the red carpet.

"What do you say to a family dinner when we get home?" Dave asked Samantha. "You know, so we know exactly where our kids are the entire time we're together."

"That sounds perfect," Samantha agreed.

While Samantha and Dave said their good-byes, the Chipmunks said farewell to Miles.

"I can't believe I'm saying this," Miles told them. "But I had fun getting into trouble with you guys. I'm bummed the trip is over."

"The trip might be over, but trust me, as long as Alvin's around, we'll always get into trouble." Simon gave his brother a pointed look.

"Thanks, Si!"

Simon shook his head. "Not a compliment, Alvin."

"Let's hang out this weekend," Theodore suggested.

"How's Friday?" Miles suggested. The

Chipmunks each gave him a high five. "I'll see you back home."

Once Miles and Samantha were gone, Alvin turned to Dave. "Admit it, you're a little sad to see the adventure end."

"Not at all," Dave grumbled. "Come on, let's go home."

Simon leaned into Alvin and asked, "Should we remind him we're still on the No Fly List?"

"Definitely not," Alvin whispered back.

Almost a week later, when their rental car pulled up in Los Angeles, Dave had one last stop to make.

"This does not look like home," Theodore said, staring out the window at a big stone building.

"It's not," Dave told him. "There's one

more important thing we have to do before we go home."

"We've been driving for days, Dave," Alvin said. "Can't it wait?"

Dave shook his head and got out of the car. "Unfortunately not. The courthouse is closed tomorrow."

"Courthouse?" Alvin squeaked. "Are we going to jail?"

"We didn't mean to cause an emergency landing, Dave!" Simon said.

"Dave," Alvin said, "does this look like a face that will survive prison?"

Dave grinned but said nothing. He just beckoned Alvin, Simon, and Theodore to come inside.

A few minutes later, he and the Chipmunks stepped into a judge's chambers. A friendly-looking judge sat behind a desk, looking through some papers. "Dave Seville?" he asked, glancing up.

"Yep, that's me."

The judge pushed the papers toward Dave. "By signing this," he said, "you agree not only to take care of, but to provide for the health, welfare, and educational needs of . . . Alvin, Simon, and Theodore."

Dave nodded. "I do."

"Alvin, Simon, and Theodore," the judge said. "Do you agree to this adoption?"

"Adoption?" Alvin asked, looking up at Dave hopefully.

"That's why we're here?" Simon said.

"You're . . . adopting us?" Theodore said, his big eyes on Dave.

"You guys were right," Dave said. "Even though you think of me as your dad and I love you just like you're my own sons, it's never been official. So I figured . . . let's make it official."

Alvin, Simon, and Theodore had tears in their eyes.

The judge interrupted their tender moment. "Chipmunks . . . ?" he asked. "Okay, well, uh, I still need you to say something like 'I agree.' To make it legal."

"I agree!" said Alvin.

"Me too!" Theodore said.

"One thousand percent," Simon added. "And that's not even a real number!"

"Does this mean we're Sevilles?" Theodore wondered.

The judge smiled. "On this day, David Seville has officially adopted Alvin, Simon, and Theodore as his children. You three have all the legal rights of any natural children . . . er, chipmunks. I hereby sign this order confirming this adoption. Congratulations!"

*   *   *

Back home, the Chipmunks couldn't stop testing out their new name for Dave.

"Hey, official and legal dad?" Alvin asked as he rolled his luggage up to the front door.

"Yes, official and legal son?" Dave replied.

"Thanks for being the best official and legal dad, Dad." Alvin smiled.

"And you three are the best official and legal sons an official and legal father could ask for." Dave unlocked the door, and then added, "Honestly, guys, this is the happiest day of my life. Literally nothing could ruin it."

Dave opened the door and stopped short.

The house was destroyed. The three squirrels in Chipmunks shirts stopped gnawing and chewing the furniture long enough to glance at Dave. Then they resumed their chewing.

Alvin gulped. "Totally forgot about this." He smiled up at Dave, hoping the happiest day of their lives wouldn't be ruined by a little stand-in squirrel destruction.

But even as their legal and official dad, Dave wasn't going to go easy on the Chipmunks. Some things would *never* change.

"Al-*viiiiiiiin!*"